Spending and Saving

Published in the United States of America by Cherry Lake Publishing
Ann Arbor, Michigan
www.cherrylakepublishing.com

Content Adviser: Danielle Peart, CPA
Reading Adviser: Cecilia Minden, PhD, Literacy expert and children's author
Book Design: Jennifer Wahi
Illustrator: Jeff Bane

Photo Credits: © pingdao /Shutterstock.com, 5; © Monkey Business Images/Shutterstock.com, 7; © Daria
Chichkareva/Shutterstock.com, 9; © Eakachai Leesin/Shutterstock.com, 11; © Hurst Photo/Shutterstock.com, 13;
© VGstockstudio/Shutterstock.com, 15; © Nattanan Zia/Shutterstock.com, 17; © LumineImages/Shutterstock.com,
19; © Indypendenz/Shutterstock.com, 21; © AVAVA/Shutterstock.com, 23; Cover, 1, 6, 12, 20, Jeff Bane

Library of Congress Cataloging-in-Publication Data

Names: Colby, Jennifer, 1971- author.
Title: Spending and saving / by Jennifer Colby.
Description: Ann Arbor : Cherry Lake Publishing, [2018] | Series: My guide to
    money | Includes bibliographical references and index.
Identifiers: LCCN 2018003319| ISBN 9781534128965 (hardcover) | ISBN
    9781534130661 (pdf) | ISBN 9781534132160 (pbk.) | ISBN 9781534133860
    (hosted ebook)
Subjects: LCSH: Finance, Personal--Juvenile literature. | Saving and
    investment--Juvenile literature. | Money--Juvenile literature.
Classification: LCC HG179 .C6568 2018 | DDC 332.024--dc23
LC record available at https://lccn.loc.gov/2018003319

Printed in the United States of America
Corporate Graphics

About the author: Jennifer Colby is a school librarian in Michigan. She saves for her retirement.

About the illustrator: Jeff Bane and his two business partners own a studio along the American River in Folsom, California, home of the 1849 Gold Rush. When Jeff's not sketching or illustrating for clients, he's either swimming or kayaking in the river to relax.

Do you have money? You can do two things with it. You can **spend** it. You can save it.

You spend money when you buy things.

People spend money all the time. They spend it on what they need, like food. They spend it on what they want, like toys.

You save money when you do not spend it.

What do you save your money for?

It is smart to save money. Some people save money for vacations. They save money for a house.

Some people also save money for an **emergency**.

The money you save can **earn** more. It can earn **interest**.

Your bank will pay you interest on money you save.

You make money from the interest! That is smart saving.

Do you have money saved in a bank? If you do, you earn interest! You make more money by saving more.

glossary

earn (URN) to get

emergency (ih-MUR-juhn-see) a sudden and scary problem that requires action

interest (IN-trist) money paid to you by a bank for keeping your savings there

spend (SPEND) to use up money by buying things

index